DE _ _

ANYONE
WHO READS
THIS

HUGH HOWEY
AND ELINOR TAYLOR

This journal was found as-is
I take no responsibility for writing it
or you reading it

If it resembles anything that seems
familiar to you, then maybe you're
to blame-

Dear Diary,

I had no idea how much of an apocalypse was spent looking for food. When you live in a walled-off store, the challenge is how to turn Kraft macaroni into something different every day. Now that I'm wandering the wastelands like all the other (un)lucky survivors, my days are like one long Easter egg hunt, but with canned goods instead of chocolates.

It reminds me of looking at apartments with Mike: walk through other people's homes, open all the cabinets and drawers, admire the ceiling height in this one, the south-facing windows in that one, step over a few bodies—

I miss the way things were. Not just the stupid canoe on the roof of my Costco, having endless paperbacks to read, but the times before that. Complaining about rent. Arguing over what to order for dinner.

Day ten since my great escape. I'm starving to death. Inside another ransacked apartment I step over two bodies and open a drawer to find a stack of old menus. It's wild what gets me sobbing these days.

-Rita

Major insight from nearly getting killed and then reading about someone's past pain: A scared little girl rummages around an apartment feeling hungry, and she thinks things are bad. She has no idea how bad things can get.

And it hits me, as I sit here bleeding out, scratching down thoughts in a journal while the woman I killed watches: what if I'm doing the same thing? What if this is an endless cycle of suffering that spirals worse and worse?

Instead of feeling sorry for myself, maybe I should feel sorry for my future self.

Things keep getting worse. That's the lesson of these end-times: they won't stop ending. Enjoy today while you still can.

Date: _____

To anyone reading this...

If we've spoken before I strongly recommend you forget all I've said previously. Don't imagine this place to be any kind of paradise. I may have exaggerated a little about that. To search for me would be a bad idea. A REALLY bad idea.

God, the mistakes are so obvious to me now. Setting myself up for trouble, inviting it in. New rule: write it down, keep it hidden. If this ends the way I suspect it might, only afterwards would my words be found.

Better. Safer that way.

Okay, so the first page of this diary is a new beginning. A fresh start for us both in which I try not to embellish and you pretend not to judge me on my bad decisions.

Here's the thing: Someone found me. They got inside my home. I thought it was rats but I was wrong. I thought it was a fog monster but I was wrong about that too.

Dear Costco, I've been wrong about so many things.

—Rita

The dead woman's blood is all over this journal. There's blood everywhere. Her blood. My blood. Mixing. An office desk with a jar full of pens. I picked one out, hand trembling. Unsure.

Weird that I feel like writing instead of running. Writing instead of tightening the t-shirt wrapped around this grisly wound. Not even sure what to write. What's the point of a journal? And who the hell wrote all this nonsense on the other pages? A voice from the past. Back when people were wistful and hopeful. Before they got blown to bits.

The woman is staring at me. A face so familiar, I know it almost as well as my own. I debate about closing her eyes, like they do in the movies. Used to think that was to give the dead some peace. But it's not for them, it's for us. We do it to not be seen. Can't handle that vacant stare.

I've got to get this bleeding stopped.

Date: _____

Hard to think with a calorie deficiency, but today's bright idea is to get out of town. I started north mostly because the wind was pushing the other way. Hitting the outskirts of town, and it's better already. I'm having more luck searching cars on the highway than I did the apartment blocks. So many people grabbed food and jumped in their cars when the clouds fell from the sky. Spent the last of their days in gridlock. Bumper to bumper asphyxiation. I make a little fire on the center line between a Toyota and a Kia and heat up a can of tomato paste. Corpses with hands at 10 and 2 staring lifelessly ahead. My kid's an honor student. Honk for Jesus.

This was the highway my mom took when she drove me off to college. Is that where I'm heading? Trying to regress? Back to the last place I can remember being happy?

Any direction is as good as another. Away from the fog. Upwind. Following the traffic.

A warning about going back to college: it won't make you younger, and you'll probably feel stupid when you get there. Trust me. My second time at college was nearly the death of me.

The bleeding has stopped. Mostly. The dead woman is still glaring at me. If she knew my mom, she wouldn't waste her afterlife with the guilt trip. I've had worse. But still ... her death hits different. I trusted her. Loved her? There are little bits of me inside that keep breaking with each new horror. I feel something crack in there. Okay, so the guilt trip is working. Damn.

Maybe this is my graduation. Have to learn how to sacrifice a life to save my own. Wish I'd known this earlier. I would've gotten out of my rotten marriage the day it died instead of years after.

Fine, here's something I learned at college the second time around: trust your nose. When things go off, get rid of them. Those leftovers in the tiny fridge aren't gonna magically freshen up.

I'm an idiot. A journal is as good a place as any to admit this, isn't it? This tiny plastic lock will keep my admissions safe. The Pink Power Princess won't tell anyone.

It's been a week since I escaped from Costco when I see a balloon drifting overhead, and I realize precisely how stupid I was. Of course if you see that you're gonna go investigate. It's not like everyone else out here had their own fully-stocked little (actually, not so little) castle of supplies to hole up in. They were staggering around hungry like I am now. I knew I had it good in there, but I had no idea how bad it was out here.

Seeing this balloon fills my head with thoughts:

A) I miss my hot tub
B) There's all kinds of food on aisle 9
C) My desire to write to "no one in particular" almost ended me
D) The asshole who stole my throne is now sending out his own balloons
E) Fuck Rita, how many people are you gonna get killed?

Oh, now she gets it. Wild watching the wheels grind together. That's right, Rita, you created a monster. Gave him the recipe. Nothing more enticing than a helpless damsel in a fully-stocked shopping center. Of course, nothing is ever quite what it seems, is it? Don't judge a book by its cover and all that.

My injuries may, as it turns out, not quite kill me. The bleeding has stopped. Mostly. Thinking on the balloons that have gotten so many people killed, thinking on the asshole writing his little missives.

I've got a pocket full of his postcards, taken off the dead body of someone who tried to warn me. Tried to warn me not to trust others. As I slowly come back to life in a building full of the dead, I have an idea. Return to sender, motherfucker. Return to sender.

Rain. Warm and heavy. I strip down and let it soak me to the skin, scrub with the foam side of a window cleaner pulled from a Chevy Volt, get the stink off. Putting my clothes back on in the back seat is a kind of contortionist yoga. I imagine an entire class doing it with me, women in the back seats of every wrecked and parked car on the highway. Allright, lift your hips! Underwear on backwards! Good job! Now take them off and let's do it again, girls!

After the rain, and somewhat predictably, the fog bank rolls in across the fields and I watch it, waiting for it to reach me before I crank up the windows and bed down for the night.

There were so many misconceptions and unfounded fears about the end of the world before it actually happened. And when you think about it, what they meant by end of the world was really just the end of people. The world, believe me, will be just fine. It's wet and warm here. Good luck keeping the mold and mildew from covering this joint.

My breath fogs the glass as I write this. Cotton clouds obscure the world until it's just me and my journal in a dim white glow. Life finds a way. It may not know where it's going, but it finds a way.

-Rita

PS: Why am I signing these? Old habits, I guess.

Life finds a way right up to the end, Rita. I was in a car wreck once, and time slowed down so much that seconds felt like hours. It's like my brain revved up to look for a way to survive, a way out, a way to avoid injury. The end of a bad relationship feels somewhat similar. Those broken months stretch out to decades. Gears spinning, searching for an escape.

Makes me wonder... if our brains can do this in a traffic accident, what about our thoughts when we die? Those moments just before we clock out? Maybe they speed up so fast that the last moments feel like a lifetime.

Okay, this is me trying not to be afraid of death. And not my own death, but the ones I've caused by my own hand. Maybe all those people still feel alive, trapped in the moment before their eyes glass over, seeing everything they've ever wanted to see.

This can't possibly be true, but I choose to believe it anyway.

Fire time is writing time. All day long I walk and forage and scurry into a hiding place when I hear any kind of noise. All day long I think "this is definitely going in the journal." And then, by the time night falls and I start a fire to warm up a can-o'-somethin', I don't really know what to write. My thoughts in the moment, I suppose. Watching the flames dance. The crackle and the pop.

How many preppers made it a priority to learn to make fire? No need, my dudes. Lighters still exist. Boxes of matches still sit unstruck in people's kitchen cabinets and glove boxes. Not once have I had to rub two sticks together. It was a fetishism, a fantasy, grown men playing Cub Scouts. What they should've learned was the fine art of writing to oneself. Now that's how you keep from going insane.

You weren't writing to yourself, Rita, you were writing to the future. To everyone who came across your postcards and now your journal. Writing across time.

Matter of fact, it occurs to me that time travel stories aren't about time at all. They're about regret. Mistakes made. The fantasy that we could go back and do it all over again, but not fuck it up this time.

Going over the way things went down, I see now how I could've done better. Been smarter. Fucked up a lot less. Got fewer people hurt. Including myself.

Circling back to a place I came close to dying might strike some as idiotic, but this is the most sure of myself I've been in ages. This is my time travel story. This is where I go back and make things worse by trying to make them better. It's where I go to murder my regrets.

Oftentimes when scavenging I find guns. The farmhouse off the northbound highway is no different. These people hung theirs on the walls, seven or eight at last count, rifles and shotguns, mostly. I wouldn't know what to do with one of those. Did it give them a sense of security? Or did they display them like that 'cause they were so goddamn afraid?

The only gun I have is the one I took from the woman in the alleyway with the needle in her arm, and the only reason I took that was out of a sense of self-preservation. A panicked reflex as the footsteps approached. I pulled her over me, let the rank juices of her decomposition trickle down my neck, until the footsteps faded and I was able to crawl out again.

I try not to think about her. Not the vile state of her, just the sadness of knowing it wasn't the disaster, the fog monsters, the bad leftover people, or anything else that brought about her demise. And that me, you, them, all of us left are merely one sore memory, one bad decision, one unbearable day from ending up the same way.

I can't tell if the gun fires and don't wish to test it in case it draws others to me. But it's small, compact, like a girl gun if ever such a thing existed. It doesn't weigh me down, more's the point.

If I need it, I'll find out if it works.

Funny to read a story about a girl traveling north while I take the same highway south. I like to think about us passing each other and giving a wave. As if that were possible. As if she weren't dead. As if I really were something rising up from the ashes.

Rita off to college for the second time, scratching her thoughts down. I want to skip ahead and see how it ends, but I've promised myself not to. One page at a time. Filling up the blank sides left empty. Maybe this is where the really dark secrets are meant to go, round the other side where no one is supposed to look. Buried deep, under lock and key.

The gun I carry is big and I know it works. Left a bruise on my shoulder the first time I fired it. Keep thinking how badly it needs a name. God knows it's done more for me than anyone I ever dated or loved. Saved my ass. Makes me feel safe. I've got no shoulder to cry on anymore, but a wooden stock does just fine.

I've lost track of days but it's probably, if we're talking old school calendar days, approaching two weeks since I left the store. (Left? Ha! Talk about euphemism). The main shift in my perception of things the further I go is that the fog is not my enemy. Quite the contrary. I'm tending to walk further, stay on the move longer, when visibility is at its worst.

Nice not to be seen. Nice to be the one doing the creeping up and around. Two can play at that game, you sons of bitches.

I've decided not to fear the unknown and I fully expect my brain to get the memo on that any time now. Meanwhile, I'm traveling with the breeze which works in my favor, keeping me at the edge of the rolling cloud for longer. If I'm going in the direction I think I am, then the state line shouldn't be far. And on the other side, St Margaret hospital. Might be able to stock up on pain meds, happy pills (better be extra strong), in the unlikely event the shelves haven't been stripped bare.

Risky.

Still, definitely worth a shot.

Rita, signing off.

State line. I'm two days from that very place, heading in the opposite direction. These lines on maps make even less sense now, and they didn't make much sense in the beforetimes.

Born on one side of a line, and you have to stay there for the rest of your life. Speak that language. Believe that religion. A jackpot and a curse might be a stone's throw apart. Takes a lot of courage to gather up your family and walk across some imaginary line, knowing how much the people on the other side don't want you there.

I wish the lines were on the ground at least, big black cartoon slashes of paint. Where we could see them. Have to step over them. Pretend it's all real.

And not just something we made up because we're scared of anyone who doesn't look like us.

Another common misconception: no electronic devices at the end of the world.

Incorrect. They are everywhere, and the ones that run on removable batteries turn out to be the best.

I found a portable CD player yesterday. Rather not say where I found it, only that I thanked the person it was on. Must've left it running (Journey's Greatest Hits), because the batteries were dead. But batteries are in every rummaged bag where cans of food should be. And lots of cars have selections of CDs.

Currently I'm listening to show tunes. What I wouldn't give to be able to belt out full volume Don't Cry For Me, Argentina, or Defying Gravity as I stroll down the longest parking lot in the universe. The end-times equivalent of cranking the car stereo up and waking the neighborhood. A pleasant distraction from the smell.

Not advisable, mind you. My voice, while not the best, would come out sounding a whole lot like a dinner bell to those hiding out around here.

Maybe save it for Broadway.

Found a Vespa in some bushes on the side of the highway, like it'd been stashed there. Probably thought they were coming back for it. Or maybe it was stashed recently and they are. No way to tell.

I transferred gas from a pickup using a jerry can. All the gas we left behind has gotten old, stale. Happens fast. But the octane booster bottles seem to wake it up. One bottle per tank. Engine knocks, but the engines on these little things always knocked. Robust as hell.

Not sure how long it'll last, but I can slide through the wrecks and jams and hug the shoulder. Must look sinister on this little thing, gun strapped to my back, hand wrapped in a bloody rag, Oakleys hiding my eyes, a murderous grin on my face.

Don't need the tunes when you've got wind in your ears.

Up until recently the fog and I had an understanding, a simpatico relationship, but I feel a shift, like it no longer has my back. I'm looking over my shoulder every mile marker now and dare not pause too long in the open else it lifts suddenly and I'm faced with what's left behind.

There's movement off the highway. Eyes watching from the cars. At least, I think.

We've avoided each other so far, the monsters and I. Part of me wondered if they sensed something in me — a kinship? A risk? A pointless exercise? — enough to make me not worth the trouble.

Today's fog isn't the pea-soup kind. We're talking middle-distance depth of vision these last couple of days. I see them and they see me. I know because the moves of those lumbering, shifting shapes are quite deliberate and mirror my own.

I'm almost into the next town, can see a big blue H for the hospital exit. A place where people go to get better. Ironic then that this might be the last thing I write. Every entry could be my last.

But what's the alternative? Live on the road among the cars for all eternity? Worse fates, I'm sure.

—Rita

It's fun speculating about what's in the fog. I've heard my share of theories by now. Here's what I think: I think we tinkered with the air and made it impossible to breathe. Killed off most. Left some with little in reserve. Those are the folks who get winded in the fog. Slow down. Fall asleep and never wake up again. They're not the ones to watch out for. The victims. The prey.

But eight billion people and lord knows how many animals, and some are built differently. Some can survive in there. Thrive, even. But it's changing them. Or the oxygen deprivation makes them hungry for something else.

Maybe our blood has what they need? All that hemoglobin. The iron. The energy they crave. Or maybe I've seen too many vampire movies.

Lived with someone like that, once. Sucked me dry. The only cure to their depression was to milk the joy out of me, one little barb and slice at a time. They did it so slowly I didn't know I was dying. Kinda like how we fucked up the earth. Slow, slow, slow . . . then all at once.

Or maybe . . . those aren't even monsters in the fog. Any more than the rest of us are.

Not a day goes by that I don't think of the fucker killing people with my words. And not a day goes by that I don't avoid writing about it.

He was so much bigger than me. Dressed like a hunter in camo and orange, which seems fitting given the way he stalked the balloons, the way he gathered up my words like rabbits, prizes to be kept.

I knew that store so much better than him. Six months better. Knew all the places to hide, which aisle floors creaked when you stood on them. I thought I had the advantage for a while there. Imagined I could find a way to drive him out, get my home back, win the unwinnable. But such thoughts were folly. Should've listened to my instincts on that and ran while I first had the chance. Not hung around to play a rigged game against someone who cared nothing for the rules.

Like I said, diary, he was so much bigger than me. Inherently strong. As patient as these empty days are long. And when the time came to find me you'd better believe he did it with ease.

—Rita

Hide and seek. I know the game well. Most of my life I've spent hiding from others. Mostly my thoughts. Doubts about relationships. Doubts about myself.

Doubts are dangerous things to hide away. They grow stronger in the dark. Like mushrooms. Like cowards. Like the things in the fog — what you think will starve them just empowers them.

Doubts are best killed early and often. Strangled in the crib.

I remind myself of this as I head south. Every step, another doubt. They crunch under my boots like brittle bones.

Five reasons to be cheerful:

One: Tiniest hint of blue in the sky this morning. Only for a moment but I'll take what I can get.

Two: I've decided to free my boobs and ditch the bra. Using it instead to strap up my ankle, which is bothering me again. Wes, you'd be impressed. (With the ankle not the boobs.)

Three: The stench of corpses in the hospital wasn't as bad as expected. Is it fading? Am I getting used to it? Either way, it's a win.

Four: Pocketed a shit ton of meds from one of the locked wards, along with a book on drugs explaining what they are, what they're for, which not to mix with which, and so on. Smashed my way in. The pills are all out of date now, naturally, but I never trusted those dates anyway. Always felt made-up. Like predicting when the world would end.

Five: The capitol is a day's walk from here, give or take. Perhaps that's where I'm headed. I'll sleep a while, leave early, and might stop off at a Holiday Inn or similar nearby. Somewhere with rooms to spare and an exit route, two sets of stairs to choose from. Always helps to have options.

Quick question, Apocalypse: was the blue sky a sign things are getting better? Guess we'll have to see what tomorrow brings.

-Rita

Names. Names are how we carry the dead. A neat little box to put them in. As if a few letters could hold so much.

I've kept people alive by saying their names. Writing them down. Even the ones I wished dead long, long ago. Kept them alive to haunt me. Gotta put an end to that.

Instead of filling these pages with ghosts, I'm gonna tell myself what I mean to do. Look forward, not back.

The plan is all right here in these pages, spelled out in neat little ruled lines with pretty handwriting. There's a menace out there hurting people. Maybe I'll feel better once he's gone. One less name in the world.

More balloons overhead. The cards dangling underneath them look like worms on hooks, wriggling for any poor dumb fishes to bite. Worms with my handwriting, or close enough. He's got the hang of it. Practiced it. Made it his. I taught him that.

Got to stop thinking about it. There's more than enough blame to go around. I'd love to spread some of my own, point a few fingers. I reached the Capitol last night and had an idea what I ought to do. Time to set off and explore, see if the local rags in the newsstands printed anything those last days, or if a dumb politician left some notes behind.

My theory is all this has something to do with the rockets they sent up, and our governor was there that day. He signed the bill. Gotta be a clue somewhere around here. Everyone else is looking for food or someone to hurt. I might be the only one with real questions.

Balloons and rockets. What other foolish things have we sent into clouds?

Oh, Rita. All the things you could've done differently. Shall I let you in on a secret? It feels like you're to blame because you are. You did the thing that led to the thing and now you feel bad. Funny how that works.

Say it with me: Your fault.

Admit it. Own it. Shout it loud and proud. That's what I do, and it feels fucking great.

Denial is a cage that traps us, locks us up. Only the truth can set us free.

I wish you could see me, standing in the middle of the highway, gun resting on the roof of a Hyundai Kona, sights lined up on a man that I know would hurt me if I gave him the chance.

BLAM.

A punch to the shoulder.

Yeah, it hurts. Yeah, I did it.

After, I scream in rage at what I've become. Hear me. I don't give a fuck.

I scaled a fire escape this evening. A balloon had tangled itself up in the railings on the third floor, the postcard still attached and flapping about in the breeze. Was it my curiosity? Or did I want to disarm one of his traps?

The climb and the anticipation of what I'd find had my heart thumping. I assumed it was one of his, but what I found were my own words. A card I had written some months back, scratching out agoraphobia after I spelled it wrong.

My nostalgia for better times was short-lived. When I flipped the card, I found more writing on the reverse! On the picture side of the card — scrawled on the white space surrounding an image of the most beautiful clear sky over a calm blue lake — some idiot had gone and replied! What is this, pal, USP fucking S?

I might have actually shouted at it, I'm not sure. He'd seen my tactic and used it to send me a message back. Must've waited for the wind to turn. 'Dear Rita,' it said. 'I'm coming to find you.' And I wanted to yell through the postcard to this man, to scream at him: No, no, turn back, save yourself. I'm not there anymore. But what would be the point? It's not as if he could hear me.

I read it a half dozen times, held it to my chest then read it again. This poor idiot. This Matthew from Queens. Whoever he is or was. Nothing more now than a fish on a hook.

They're not your problem to fix, you know. The lost men ensnared by your words. You started it, yes. But is it up to you to end it? That's some egotistical bullshit, right there.

How much control do we have on an individual scale? We think we're in charge of our own destinies, and in days past we'd balk at companies that told us – THAT ACTUALLY TOLD US – we were being manipulated. Remember that? Those were the good times.

Gotta keep posting those pictures though, right? Eyeballs and clicks, baby. Eyeballs and clicks. Just like you had to keep writing those postcards. Nothing changes but the weather. Or the fog in our case.

So, might I suggest we let Matthew from Queens (and all those others who believe they decide their own fate) deal with the fallout of your need to be seen. And, lady? Word to the wise: perhaps look a little closer to home before thinking it's your job to save everyone else.

Good news / Bad news kinda day.

First some bad news: Someone (or something) was tracking me today. Thought it was all in my head, but nope. Running on a bum ankle is no bueno.

Good news: The apartment building I ducked into looks like a good place to bed down. A mere stone's throw from the capitol buildings. It's clean enough — the room I'm in is corpse-free and smells only mildly foul.

Bad news: Whoever it was outside must've seen me come in here. I tried scaring them off, told them I was armed and held my little gun into the air, then looked like the world's biggest moron when all it did was go clicky-click-click. Come on, Apocalypse. Give me a break.

Good news: They didn't kill me on the spot when the gun failed. Didn't approach me at all in fact. Weird, don't you think? I'm sitting here with the curtains drawn trying to figure out why and if I'm safe to close my eyes even for a little while. I must, though. Big day tomorrow, and the mist is thickening up again. Which I suppose answers my question about things getting better. The answer being a resounding no.

Good news / Good news / Good news kinda day.

The good news is that I'm on the edge of town, which means back in the meat grinder. More survivors lurking about to worry over. More dudes with more guns. More sleeping by day and moving at night. More discomfort, more shots fired, more bruises on my shoulder, more dead people to walk past, staring at me as they enjoy their eternity of thoughts.

The second bit of good news is that I no longer believe in bad news. Nothing bad truly happens. It's just stuff. Molecules bouncing into molecules. Chemical reactions. The laws of physics. Sure, we feel things. Some of those things aren't wonderful. But it's just cues from the environment to do something different. To act. Nothing but good news if you're still alive to get any kind of news at all.

Third piece of good news: I found a name for my rifle. Buck. Because he kicks like a horse trying to throw its rider. Easy, girl. I got you. And I got him. And him. And that fucker over there, too.

The layout of the town is coming back to me like chapters in a book I once read, vague but familiar. I know these streets, the park with the fountains, this square I'm in, with its scented gardens. where old people and college students ~~go to hang out~~. Used to hang out. Dammit.

We'd perch on the low walls bordering the roses and sip coffee or lick drippy ice cream out of sugar cones. These gardens aren't manicured now like when I lived here. It's been some years since any care was shown to the roses, longer still since my college days, and the grass is up to my thighs. But who gives a rat's ass?

Speaking of which, there'll be little scurrying animals in those grasses who'll be loving this. Good for them, I say. It's your turn now. Live your best lives, stuff your faces and procreate like it's going out of style. Take over and run this place. We could and did do worse.

A word of advice though, my furry friends: When you reach that peak of existence and become the apex sentient overlords of planet Earth, when you look up (as you will; we all do) and decide that you know better than the accumulated wisdom of the ages, that you can rebalance what you've thrown out of kilter with the simplest of tweaks, please consider the possibility — and I mean this with love — that you're actually full of crap.

It's wild how words can wake you from a slumber. How much of life is sleep-walking from one habit to another, wearing a groove in the Earth as we shuffle through the familiar. Something about this entry on the other side of my pen, about places where people used to do things and now don't, the voids we leave behind—

I realize now how empty the world is without us. Yes, the animals will inherit the earth. Yes, we were poisoning the land, the seas. Yes, we drove so much extinct. Yeah, we kinda fucked up.

But no one else ever wrote poetry to this place. No one painted it like we did. Sat at the rim of a canyon and wept for the beauty of it all. There must be a billion worlds out there full of life without a single creature wise enough and dumb enough to weep over what they've ruined.

We will always have that. We lifted ourselves just high enough to see how great it all was. And no higher.

In my dreams, I heard a baby crying last night. Then I woke up and the noise was still there, coming from the direction of my old college campus. Two or three blocks away and its tiny voice pierces the quiet, echoes through the light mist even as I sit here writing by the faint sunrise. Must be hungry. If I thought someone would feed me, I'd make the same noise. I hear you, little dude. I hear you.

Can't believe I'm writing this but I'm toying with checking it out. Crazy the thoughts hunger inspires. You get so starved that living becomes secondary to eating. Absurd risks seem reasonable. Hobbling around like I am, I cover less ground for looting purposes. So my brain says, "where there's a baby there's a family, and where there's a family there's food, maybe enough for me."

If they're the type to shoot through the door without checking out the window, I might die a fool. But I can live with that. Live. Heh.

Better get going. My stomach thinks my throat's been cut.

Slowly realizing how much this journal means to me. Caught myself in the middle of the day thinking about what I'd write tonight, then realized how many days I've been doing just that - planning what I'd write later to no one in particular.

My god, we all need someone to talk to, don't we. Go crazy otherwise. I compose entries in my head, a hundred for each one I actually write. Doesn't matter how exhausted I am, how dark it is, that I've got nothing important to say, just that I need to say something to someone.

I guess that's what the postcard nonsense is all about, isn't it. For the guy doing it now, it might be a lure, but I bet even for him it serves the same purpose. We aren't meant to be alone. Our ears aren't meant for only our voices.

Bullets zing overhead. A group of three or four are hoping they'll get lucky, taking potshots at the flicker of my lighter as I make today's entry. Settle down, boys. I'm writing over here.

Took me a moment to realize what I was seeing. At first, it was just a flash. Then the pattern repeated. Sure enough: SOS. Coming from the top floor of a highrise dormitory. Went to a party in that building once. Now someone else is beckoning.

Not falling for that. I walked on and ignored the torch bait and only the smallest part of me wondered if I just let someone die.

The feeling passed. Not enough space in this little book or in my head for guilt. On the balance of probabilities it was a trap. Doesn't take me many times saying so before I start to believe it, and the regret I'm not supposed to be feeling withers and leaves me to more important thoughts.

Like the banging drums. Another hazard. I hear them and know I ought to steer around them but they move with the wind, always just ahead, blocking my way. And I get the sense I'm being corralled.

Fear and hope. I remember not too long ago being corralled by such things. The fear of dying, the hope of salvation, twin forces guiding me through the world.

I don't feel like me anymore. Something snapped. I'm pretty sure I know when. Like a baptism of blood, went in one person and came out something different.

I feel calm now. I move steady through this world. When I stand up and prop Buck on the roof of a car, I don't even flinch at the shots ringing out. Because these fuckers fire at me with fear and hope. They are scared of me, and they think luck will guide their aim.

Doesn't work that way. I don't move an inch. Exhale. Frozen in place. Little X lined up on a trembling soul trying to kill me. Think of the glass bottles I've practiced on. Fragile little necks explode back into sand. Dust to dust.

Squeeze the finger. Slowly. Fear and hope are old friends, long since dead. Now I just feel my purpose.

There's a group ahead, at least a dozen? Can't see them, only smell the campfire and hear the voices, the cackling laughter and drums. How sure I was that they were drawing me in. But now I doubt myself. Paranoia getting the better of me after weeks on the road and a handful of close calls. All the same, I'm hanging back until I get a clearer view of them. They sound full-bellied and happy which makes me question what they did to be that way.

Barbeque. That's what I can smell. A familiar vibe, like August gatherings in the park, bare feet on the grass, beers chilling in a crate in a slow moving stream, the latest tunes filling the air, drifting out from a car radio as love-struck couples lie on their backs, stroke each others arms, and give meaning to clouds.

Joyous is how it would've felt in days gone by. Worrisome is what it is now.

I know from the tightness in my gut that these are not my people and that I should veer sharply away, avoid all contact. I also know I need to get the measure of them, the danger they pose. So I creep forward, sheltering behind street furniture and fire hydrants and in doorways, until I get close enough to see what I'm dealing with. Jot down a few notes here.

Shit — the drumming just stopped.

Question for car manufacturers: why do you make the overhead lights a freakin' Mensa puzzle? I feel like a chimpanzee in some of these cars, poking the ceiling, twisting the turn signal, rolling up the little dimmer wheel until it clicks, whatever magical combination gets a light to come on instead of a sunglass holder to fold down.

Label your buttons, people.

One thing I will say, modern car batteries are built well. Pretty much every car still has a little juice in it. Enough to write a journal entry by, or see to rummage through my pack for the least disgusting thing to eat, or to pop on the radio and chill to the static.

Something about airwave static that used to annoy me but I now find comforting. It's quieter than silence, somehow. Is anything louder than complete silence? If you dismiss this question, you've never been in a place without even a whisper of noise.

Lucky you.

My flashlight survived the fall, which means I can at least write about how I'm going to die. At the bottom of an elevator shaft. Like a fool.

When the drumming stopped, so too did the laughter and conversation. And let me tell you, just like how storm chasers warn that if a tornado appears not to be moving, it's probably coming right at you, silence is fucking scary when you know you aren't alone. Silence and stillness — I trust neither. I wasn't taking chances. I turned tail, ran inside the nearest dorm, down an open hallway that got darker and darker, until the open elevator door gobbled me up.

Twenty or thirty feet, it felt like. Onto a pile of old bunk bed mattresses several layers deep — the only reason I didn't break my head. The elevator shaft walls have been stripped bare of wire and cable and anything to climb. The stench of motor oil and grease, which covers every surface. A bucket in the corner that's mostly empty, but smeared with feces and reeking.

A lot of little clues that point the same direction: someone built a trap, and I fell right into it. A trap for keeping people alive. But for how long?

Rita, Rita, Rita. Painful reading this one. Thanks for taking us all back there, to your moment of pure folly. Who else will read this and laugh? Will they wonder how the hell you made it so long? How lucky one poor woman can be?

I made a promise to not read ahead. I only get to read a page of history when I sit down to write one about the present. That's the promise.

But my goodness, you make it difficult sometimes. I used to dread my tomorrows. Used to dread surviving one more day.

Now I can't wait. Took out the last of those bastards pinning me down. One had a can of corned beef hash on him. Heating that up and jotting this by the flickering flame. Almost midnight. Almost tomorrow. Love these technicalities. Fifteen or so more minutes and then I get to turn the page.

Light is a precious thing when it's your own. When you control it. Spent what felt like hours in the pitch black, covered in grease, exhausted from trying to climb my way out. Tried to sleep. Tried to listen for the drums. Or footsteps above. Tried not to think about my bladder or the bucket.

When my flashlight flickered, I realized I'm on my last set of batteries. If that goes, I'm blind down here. I'll go mad and then I'll die. Would love to die sane, please. Made it this far in life. Don't want to go out crazy in case we spend the afterlife in our most recent save-file.

A beam of light washed over me from above, a stranger in silhouette. I froze. Light is a terrifying thing when it's not your own. Hello, the person said, a little squeak of a voice. A kid. Asked me if I was alive. I wanted to make a joke, the kind of jokes dads make - couldn't tell you if I wasn't, could I?

What's your name, I asked. Can you get me out. Can you keep this a secret.

Wasn't sure if I should beg him to go get help or to never come back. There are worse things than dying alone. After the kid ran off I thought of a few, then decided to use up some flickering juice to write this down in case someone finds it someday.

-Rita.sav__final__FINAL__USE-THIS-ONE__V2

Not many people think on the afterlife, not as deep as they should. Just because we don't want to die anytime soon doesn't mean it's a good idea to live forever. Forever's a long time. A trillion years doesn't even dent it. Neither does the next trillion. Or the trillion after. Every moment that goes by is no step closer to your last.

There was a time I thought of myself as a Christian. Growing up, we never discussed these things, not really. Average American lifespan is less than eighty years. You think we'll remember any of this life after trillions and trillions and trillions of the afterlife? We won't remember what we did to get in heaven. Or why we're being punished for all eternity.

Imagine judging someone forever because of what they did in the blink of an eye.

It makes no logical sense. Even less moral sense.

If you'd asked, I would've told you I believed in a god, back before I dwelled on such things. But the more I dug into these questions, the bigger the holes I started to see. Me being me, I kept right on digging.

Dig deep enough and you get through to the other side.

Nothing to do in a cannibal cult trap but think about random shit. Here's one for ya: There was this guy who worked down at the marina at the same time as me, in the months before the rocket launch. Name was Ted. He was one of those real alpha male types, know what I mean? About as far from Mike as you're ever likely to get.

Anyhow, this Ted asked me out a few times, showed up in his sports car, said a girl like me could do a lot worse than hook up with a guy like him. I didn't bring up the fact that I was married. Weirdly it didn't seem important. I declined all the same. Something in the eyes. Something missing. Not a bad guy, this Ted, just not entirely there. Some people spend their lives trying to fill that gap, don't they? With things, other people, vices.

I think about him sometimes, wonder how he fared when it happened. All muscles and mouth. I wonder how he coped when the bodies started to pile up.

That's a lie. I don't wonder at all. I was going to be more honest so here it is: I like to imagine him being one of the first. To die, I mean. Is that terrible? I like to think of all the Teds of the world failing at life in a spectacular way. Failing at surviving and dying hungry and alone and probably crying for their mothers. Honest enough?

Or maybe I just know I don't deserve to go out like this.

~Rita

Deserve. That's a fine word right there. Like the universe owes us a damn thing.

I think most of human suffering is tied up in the mistaken belief that life is supposed to be fair, that we were put here to be happy, and anything that gets in the way of that is an injustice. I used to think this way. Life was about my own amusement. But that was a luxury of modern times and modern thinking.

People used to live their entire lives like you there in your hole, Rita. Sheltering in caves. Confined to cages. Living in one little place. Shitting in buckets. Were we ever meant to be happy? Or did we get a taste for it and that's all we ever wanted to feel again? Chasing that dragon for all it was worth.

I miss the Vespa already. How the wind on my face felt. The sense of speed and acceleration. When the tire blew out, all I could think was "life's not fair." As if it was meant to be. As if anyone built it with a plan in mind.

That fantasy is a dark well. A greased trap. Nothing to do but die down there.

A restless night of foul dreams and lost hope for getting out of this pit and I'm woken by hailstones, flung by the kid. Not hail but pellets of some kind. I sniffed one. Dogfood, I think. Didn't care, I ate it and every other one that rained down.

Water? I said, and I mimed the act of sipping from a cup. Can't see his face with his light shining in my eyes, but he scuttled off, mission accepted. An eternity passed.

Light, quick footfalls in the hallway and I was relieved to only hear one set — no adults following. Feels like I'm his secret, for now. Until whoever built this trap comes to check in on it. Or chases the next person in and they land on my head in the dark.

The kid lowers something my way. A rope. A way out. A bucket dangling on the end, sloshing with water. My mouth is cotton. Swollen from thirst. Precious water splashing over the edge, raining down on me. Precious rope for hauling myself out.

And then someone down the hallway shouts, an adult voice, and the kid startles. The bucket plunges, the rope slithering after, limp and useless in a heap.

I tried to catch the bucket. Hit my forearm, my head, went sideways, all that precious fluid dumping out, soaking the mattresses.

Licked the rim. Patted a few drops into my mouth.

Salvation gone.

Damn, Rita. If you hadn't set your story down, no one would believe it. Or know it ever happened. How many crazy stories like this will we never know about, because poor fools took the tales to their graves? Billions. Enough comic, cosmic suffering to fill endless Greek tragedies. Sisters falling in love with brothers. Lovers warring over a slight misunderstanding. Kids poisoning themselves with infatuation.

I used to have a hard time reading fiction and suspending disbelief. How could so much happen to a single protagonist? How could every bullet miss? How do they survive?

The apocalypse is teaching me the answer: We work backwards. Take any random survivor this deep into the mess, and those are the ones the bullets (mostly) missed. Those are the lucky fools. The Ritas of the world. Tell their stories backwards, and yeah it seems unlikely. But that's because they're still alive. That's what makes them the protagonist.

Now write it all down, even if there aren't enough people to read it. Even if the few who do read it don't learn a damn thing. Buckets of wisdom lowered on ropes, fumbled by those who could use it.

The drumming started up again. Flashlight batteries are so low I have to take them out, spin them, wondering why the hell that even works. The drums remind me of the smell of BBQ. It's been a few days, surely, judging by my thirst. A few days since they cooked up whoever was here last? Is this their larder? Am I livestock?

All I can think about is the water that spilled. The few drops on my tongue. Driving me mad. I bury my head into an old dorm mattress and cry quietly to myself. That's when I hear a sound — a dripping. Water dripping.

Pulling up mattress after mattress, leaning them against the grease-slathered walls, seven, eight layers deep, digging and digging, until I reach metal. Of course. All this time, I assumed the elevator car was somewhere far above, dangling on a rusted cable, ready to fall on me at any moment. I've been living on top of it.

Footsteps, coming down the hallway. People laughing. A kid's voice, squealing at some joke. While I paw for the hatch that has to be there, has to be there, is there in every movie, the hero escapes upwards, but my escape is down.

I find the handle in the dark, even as a glow of light reaches the end of the hall, flickering like a flame, coming for me.

Water dribbling through a crack. I throw my feeble strength into the handle. Mattresses falling down on me, burying me alive. So I go deeper.

A red balloon drifts overhead, floating on the breeze. I'm close enough now to be in range of the bait. Reminds me of days spent on the water with my dad, watching a little red bobber go up and down, tiny ripples radiating outward, my whole body tense for the moment it would sink and I'd give the rod a yank to set the hook.

My dad only smoked while we were fishing. Must've been a secret from Mom, I realized many years later, when I started keeping such secrets of my own. A little lie between me and him. Somehow he knew I wouldn't say anything, wouldn't even think to say anything, because what happened in that little boat had no bearing on the rest of our lives. Conversations there never made it to shore.

I hated the smell of cigarette smoke for the rest of my life, but I loved the way his breath smelled when he kissed me on the cheek, another little fish released back to the wild. His breath stank, of course. But it was his breath. And that made the difference.

I dropped into the elevator right as the voices got near, the car itself blessedly empty, and waited in the dark for them to go away. They'll probably think the kid was playing a prank. Or maybe they'll notice the mattresses are scattered and realize where I've gone and come for me. Either way, I wait until they leave to pry open the elevator door and enter the basement. Flashlight flickering. I'll be feeling my way through the dark soon, regretting every night I spent writing instead of conserving the batteries.

The laundry. There are bodies here, faces staring up that I only see for a moment when the flashlight flickers. Dead a long time. Desiccated corpses. Skulls with hollow eyes. You'd think I'd be used to seeing bodies by now, but life and death are full of surprises. Need to find the stairs. Tripping over someone who probably ran down here when the fog first settled, body falling apart underfoot, stepping through someone's ribcage, almost nothing holding us together.

So little holding me together. Bang the flashlight on the heel of my hand, knocking the light out of the damn thing, tugging on doors, wishing for those exit signs that I cursed in the cinema. Useless things. Never were going to work when we really needed them, in the time past the power.

Steps. Finally. Staggering up in the dark. I hear them shouting, looking for me. Out an emergency exit, and the promise of a fire alarm goes unfulfilled. I burst into the open air, thankful for the lack of power. I run, my mind blank, heading for a place I remember from a thousand years ago.

I knew you survived, because there are more pages. Because you had to write about your escape somewhere. But still, a part of me wondered if it would go differently this time. Maybe they'd eat you and someone else would write the next entry. Maybe the next entry would be a recipe or a Yelp review.

Rita, five stars, would eat again, paired well with rainwater.

I knew, but still I felt the fear, rising up like bile.

The power of words. Whoever is reading this, what do you feel? Can you feel the tiredness in my bones? Can you hear the crackle of my little campfire? Can you smell the anger coming through my pores as I read another one of his postcards?

Guess what happens next. I dare you.

Sitting in my old dorm, writing about the last two days and what may've been my first cannibal cult of the apocalypse. Easy to laugh about now. Hard to express the feeling of impending doom in the moment. Worse than waking up and remembering a term paper is due today.

The old dorms, like me, have seen better days. The furniture's changed a bit, the decor, but I can still hear the echoes of our college years. The pitter-patter of socked feet in the hallway. Tik Tok by Ke$ha on repeat. Francine and Linda laughing through this paper-thin wall.

Francine and Linda. They'll be dead now. Then again, they might be alive and thinking about me, assuming the worst.

Thinking of Linda reminds me of dad, not for great reasons. Her nickname was Whiplash from the way heads turned when she walked past. We laughed about it, right up until Dad came to visit and I saw he wasn't immune. I'd seen how he looked at women on the street who weren't Mom. Now my friends were those women. And it hit me like a freight train that my dad was no different than any other frat boy.

Drinking soup from a can, realizing I'm not going to die this day, writing by moonlight. I think of the men who looked at me the way Dad looked at Linda. Leering. Starving. Licking their lips. Most of those men had daughters my age, I bet.

I think it's in my old dorm room from a thousand years ago, that I regret all the guns I've passed over and left behind.

And I make a vow to pick up and learn how to use one.

Five things to know about firing a rifle in the apocalypse:

1) Never fire from the same place twice.
        Shoot and scoot.

2) Aim for the chest if possible.
        A slight miss = a light mist.

3) Reload when you can, not when you need to.
        Clicks are for dicks.

4) Don't anticipate the recoil.
        In a pinch, don't flinch!

5) Zero regrets. Pretend it's target practice.
        BOTTLE IT UP.

Couldn't sleep. We always joked about how the dorms were haunted, and I can attest that staying there alone, in the wake of the end of humankind, didn't make it feel any less plausible. Old buildings creak and groan as they cool. To which I say, no thank you. Fuck that with a cherry on top.

So I did what I shouldn't and went outside in the nighttime, crossed town in the dark. Some kid's school backpack on my back, a little food, new batteries, a bottle of gutter water. And do you know what? It felt good, liberating even. It would appear fog monsters need their sleep too, because all was quiet the whole way. No shuffling, no gunfire.

Took hardly any time to get here. From one haunted house to another. As I write this I'm sitting looking up at the capitol building waiting for the light to flash again — top floor, second window from the end. More of a glow than a flash, the slow moving aura of a candle or kerosene lamp.

There! I didn't imagine it! I'm not crazy. Not about this, at least.

And now I find myself asking the question: what's worse, thinking someone might be in there or knowing they are?

—Rita

There are pages torn out here. Regrets, tossed away. Would love to read them.

Deep down, I know there are no secrets here. This journal was found and will be found again, and even when the margins are full and there's no space to leave anything, someone will pick it up and squeeze out every last drop.

Honestly not sure if I'd still be writing if I didn't believe that. I want to be remembered. And not as I am, but how I used to be. There I go, thinking about the true end-times again. The afterlife I learned about in church. Which version of us goes there? Who gets immortalized? Because we aren't the same throughout life. I used to be playful. Cheerful. Happy-go-lucky.

I feel a despondency of late. Something that went missing with the pieces of me. And this isn't how I want to spend my eternity. I want to be the best version of me.

That's the light in my attic, flickering around somewhere. The ghost I'm haunted by is my favorite version of myself, creaking its old bones as it shuffles away and hides.

Dear Diary, I made a new friend. His name is Tony G.

Tall, intense, I'd guess late forties. A distinct lack of social skills. This morning he walked out of the mist and straight for the car I was sleeping in like we were old buds at a bar, arms out for a hug, wearing what he must've hoped was a friendly smile, but was more of a desperate grin.

Hey! Hi! How are you? Good to see you!, chattering like he'd done a line of coke. I got out of the car and grabbed my bag to bolt, but he was on me, hugged me, stank like a rotting son of a bitch, and all I could think was: this is a guy who needs antibiotics. For what, I didn't know, but some part of him sure as fuck was festering.

He told me he used to work in an office around here where there was more than one Tony. Hence the G. They're all gone now, the other Tonys, other eveyones for that matter. So no more need for the identifier. Still, he kept it. Tony G was who he was. I could tell he clung to it like the last shreds of his sanity. The G meant he wasn't alone, that there were others like him. Who was I to say otherwise?

Tony G offered me some of his rat jerky with a genuine enthusiasm that made me sad for him. I said I'd just eaten, but thanks. Better I lie than take stupid risks. Better I hurt the feelings of a stranger than die of salmonella having lasted this long. We sat as he ate like we'd done it a thousand times. He told me all kinds of things. I said very little.

Then he showed me his collection of postcards.

Fucking postcards. They've been a pain in the ass for as long as anyone can remember. Who invented the stupid things?

Spinner racks all over the world full of perfect images of touristic things that never look that good in person. Driving home the guilt of how long it's been since you've called your parents. The sadness that it's been forever since anyone wrote you. The realization that you don't have enough friends whose address you even know to go for the 3 for $5 special.

Then there's the idea that anything you could say in such limited space will ever have any meaning. Or that a note sent without an envelope through a dozen hands isn't the weirdest way to communicate. Or that the receiver isn't going to get this well after you're back home working a grind at your cubicle desk.

Postcards are the original social media: pissing off everyone, pleasing nobody, inspiring jealousy, and painting a false view of the world. Fuck yeah, I'm shooting them out of the sky.

Day two with Tony G. I break out my journal to get some "me" time and he goes through his postcards again. He holds them with a kind of reverence. His most prized possessions, almost like religious artifacts. Careful, he told me yesterday. Don't bend them or damage them or rub off the ink. He said he hadn't read them enough times yet.

When I leafed through them, some were ones I'd written, others were not. The hunter does his Fs and Ts a little differently. Some had words on the one side where either I or the hunter had scrawled my stupid thoughts, while some had messages front and back. Replies. And from more than one person.

It occurred to me then that when Tony G introduced himself, I had reciprocated. Told him my name: Rita. The same name as on those postcards, on every last one of them. Rita. And that smile of his, that desperate grin — took on a different meaning: a hunger of another sort.

Surely he doesn't think I'm the same person, right? There are lots of Ritas in the world. I'm being paranoid. Or he's being paranoid. What if we're both being paranoid?

He doesn't know. He doesn't know. He doesn't know.

Probably should stop writing my name everywhere.

Rita, Rita, Rita. It's a bit too late for that, doncha think?

Tonight I sleep beneath an underpass. It's raining, which seems to dispel the mist and annoy the things living in it. Are the dark shapes pulling away from me lately? Or am I one of the dark shapes? I forget who I am sometimes.

A few nights ago I got into a car to rummage around and bed down for the night, and the first thing I caught myself doing was adjusting the rearview. Pushing it toward the ceiling. Not wanting to see myself. Wanting to be someone else. Maybe because of the people I've killed. Maybe because I don't recognize who I've become.

There's graffiti all around me. People spraying their names all over town in big block letters. Not their real names, but who they'd like to be. VILIN. OZONE. MERMAID. I want a name like that.

The light of my fire is dying. Time for sleep. Waterfalls to either side.

Day three of my Tony G problem. I told him I wanted to sleep alone, made up a bullshit story that I suffer from anthropophobia, the fear of anyone not me. Sure, he said. No problem, he said. Woke up this morning with him standing outside the car staring through the passenger window at me.

Good morning, you weirdo. I mean, he did have instant coffee waiting. But something ain't right.

I didn't like my chances of outrunning him. So I kept my cool and played the game, the one where we know the person could lose their shit any minute now, but we bite our tongue and smile in the right places, calm it down, listen and observe and take note of their moves and their tone of voice.

There are many ways to survive. I know this the hard way.

I need to use the bathroom, I said.

As soon as I got around the side of the capitol building, I ran. I left the last of my water with him. Worth it to get away.

I ducked into a different building, one where the door hung open, barricaded it shut behind me. And as I write this, my breathing not fully back to normal yet, I hear him outside searching the streets, calling my name. Rita. Rita. Like he fucking knows me.

Surviving the apocalypse would be better with a friend. Took a bullet in the arm today (laughed out loud for a solid five minutes after writing this, the absurdity of it all, that this is my life and it's starting to feel normal). Several things about getting shot made me feel alone in a way I haven't in a long, long time.

First, saying "ouch" with nobody around kinda defeats the point. I want to let someone other than me know that I'm hurt. I already know. Ouch isn't for loners.

Second, there's nobody to discuss how unrealistic bullet wounds are on film. A lot of the time in the real world, a bullet doesn't kill anyone. They crawl around screaming and crying and begging for mercy. Takes a few rounds. This one passed right through the meat of my arm. Hurts like hell, but I didn't fall over with my eyes open waiting for the director to yell "Cut!"

Third, tying off a bandage by yourself is a major inconvenience. I need a friend to hold this first knot while I tie the second, a friend to give me a finger. Heh. Okay, now I'm laughing even harder.

The capitol building has an underground parking lot. I'm looking at it now with its roll-style security gate pulled down to block the entrance. No way I can get in the gate without bolt cutters as there's a padlock the size of my fist, so guess I'll be climbing in through a window. Keeping low, in case Tony G with his postcard collection is watching and waiting for me to return.

Every night I've seen a light at the top of this building. Part of me hopes it's Governor Merck up there, living alone, his little bunker in the sky. I remember his face on TV before the world went to shit — his weird little grin as the rockets went up, the ones meant to save us. Pretty sure they had the opposite effect, you smirking asshole.

My mom used to say that when it came to the liars of this world there was always a tell if you knew what to look for. She said Dad had it. And Mike. She told me this before I was willing to listen. She told me this before she started losing her her ability to see even the simplest of things.

Governor Merck had that look. Every time I saw his face on TV, there it was. Something missing. Maybe the job does that to people. Or maybe those are the only people who want the job. Somehow, we keep voting for them. I hope that's him up there. Would love to kick that bastard in the shin.

-Rita

P.S. Merck rhymes with smirk.

All our problems started when everything became news. 24/7/365 news. Honestly, not that much really happens. Most of life is waiting for the next thing to get our attention. Everything that needs relating can be told in a single hour, with commercials. And then again at 11 for the folks who got home late.

We used to be bored, in a good way. Time with our thoughts. With loved ones. More hours at work, occupying our anxious little brains. Then we traded the ennui for anger. We got more hours of news than what was actually happening. News became opinion, opinions differed, differences brewed and bubbled and spewed. Wars are fought over way less than this. Cancer is easier to cure.

Postcards aren't just dangerous, they are nonsense. Way too short. The Twitter of correspondence. Journals, my friend, had it all figured out. They were the 6 o'clock news of the written word. Everything you needed to know about the day's events in a few paragraphs.

Again at 11pm if you turn the page.

Holy crap.

Whoever is hiding out up there, in their wisdom, blocked the only way up. A shit-ton of furniture all bound with electrical cables and rope. Figures. They had to keep the bad guys from breaking in somehow. Looks as if some have tried, though, with bolt cutters or hacksaws. But the thicket of chairs and desks goes back a ways. Maybe all the way up the stairwell a floor or two. Must say, I do like a challenge.

(School report 2003: 'Rita's resourcefulness is matched only by her ability to care less about mathematics.')

These people have no idea who they're dealing with — I'm a born problem solver, pal — and they've piqued my interest now.

There's a stink coming from the tangled barricade. When I look deeper in I see parts of the structure that aren't made of metal or plastic or wood. Things snarled up that look to have crawled in there by themselves, died there, rotted there. People trying to find a way up and in. Or maybe down and out. Either way they failed, their corpses now serving only as a further deterrent to others who might try the same.

Others, that is, except me.

The guy I took out yesterday was well-stocked with supplies. This is the weirdest thing to get used to: rummaging through people like they are ATMs. He had a Snickers in his hip pocket, which is already in my belly. A key on one of those zip-pulls, which I'm planning on using for my pen light. Now for another bag swap.

Bag swaps are the best. A chance to rearrange and take stock. His bag was in far better shape than mine, and I've upgraded twice already. I tend to go for the one with the most pockets. I'm a sucker for pockets. I would totally go for a bag that was nothing but pockets. Inside every pocket is just more pockets. Pockets all the way down.

Reminds me of how much I hated open floor plans. Who thought that was ever a good idea? Put a kitchen in the TV room? How many divorces did that lead to? Rooms should have a purpose. Places to go so you know what for.

I'll tell you who invented open floor plans: the folks who had to build walls. Let's build fewer walls and charge people more. Genius. And then let's make the people with walls feel like losers and charge them to come knock those perfectly good walls down. More genius.

What a fucking racket. Almost as much of a racket as putting away the dishes while someone is trying to watch their game.

There's someone up there, diary, that much we know. I've seen a moving light in the top floor window. Which leaves us with a quandary: water and supplies don't last forever, certainly not in an office setting, and it's been a while since the world fell apart. Gotta get hungry sometime. So, I wondered, with the stairwell all blocked up how the hell are they getting in and out?

I spend a while walking the halls and checking the offices for any other way up. The fire escape would've been an obvious choice. But they'd detached that from the side of the building and now it lays twisted and broken in the street. The elevator shaft too is filled with debris, no way past it, not that I would want to go in there if my life depended on it. I'm so done with elevators.

Sometimes I hear Tony G outside calling my name. Wish he'd give it up. Creeps me the fuck out, puts me on edge, and I do my best to stay clear of any windows. Go deeper inside.

I noticed something then, in a small internal room I'd searched several times already, a flap of cloth sticking out from a cupboard built into a wall. It looked out of place and I wondered how I hadn't taken note of it before. I went over and tugged the cupboard handle which I found slid upwards and there it was — a vertical tunnel in the wall, a trash chute, and hanging down the center of it like the wick of an invisible candle a rope made of so many flags knotted end to end.

And all I could think was, you nifty little bastard!

Okay, this is the damnedest thing. Not sure I even trust what I saw or what I'm writing, so bear with me, future me, as you try to piece all this back together. Deep breaths. Just the facts.

A while back I learned to follow the mist when it moves, because the air seems clear behind it. Or maybe because moving with the breeze is just the safest mode of travel. Can't relate all the times I felt the mist was chasing me down dead-end alleys and into buildings with no egress. Trapping me.

Today I was following a wall of fog, saw some shapes moving at the edge, didn't take them for survivors, so I kept my rifle slung, and I realized they were moving as fast as their poor bodies could. Away from me. More importantly, away from the edge of the mist. Like they were scared. Like the clean air was overtaking them.

As the wind shifted, one of them got caught out in the clear. Writhed like it couldn't breathe and fell. Died right there. It was a man, looks normal on the outside.

What. The. Actual. Fuck.

As I look up the chute, I can see what are actually state flags knotted together to form loops at intervals, hand holds, foot holds, places to push up on, which is actually pretty smart. More of a ladder than a rope. My upper body strength is far from Ninja Warrior level, and I wasn't liking my chances of pulling myself up there, pirate-style. Looks as if I only need to climb a couple of floors, though. Perhaps that's as far as the barricade goes. Guessing I'll climb out through another sliding hatch at that point. Fourth floor, maybe? Fifth?

All's quiet up there. Now or never, right? Part two to follow if I don't fall and break my neck, or meet a gun muzzle at the top. You're going in my pocket now, diary. Wish me luck.

...okay, so I didn't die. Although halfway up the flag ladder, around Wyoming, I did start to question my life choices. I'm writing this on the landing of the tenth floor. Not seen anyone yet, but I can hear them up there. Expensive shoes on expensive flooring. The rustle of papers. My money's on it being Merck, the piece of shit. Wouldn't put it past that sleazeball saving himself and scuttling home to his kingdom after a busy day spent destroying the planet.

The only way is up.

Great, now I'll have that song in my head the rest of the day. Or until I die. Whichever comes first.

Ugh. I'm being hunted. Three or four well-equipped guys. Can't risk the light. Super annoying.

Well look at that, Apocalypse. Seems you still have a few surprises up your sleeve. Helluva day. The light fades and I sit here on Governor Merck's couch making these notes, while my gracious host picks out a fine wine to go with our dinner. Dude. WTF? This is not how I thought this would go.

After my last entry, I climbed the stairs and turned a corner onto the fourteenth floor to find a woman standing there with the same look and build as my Aunt Helen. By which I mean she rocked a cardigan and pearls. The gray hairs had long since won the battle. And there were signs on her face of a life well lived. Only, unlike my Aunt Helen, this woman had a can of pepper spray pointed at me, and her expression said she wasn't afraid to use it.

She demanded to know who I was, what I wanted, so I held my hands up and stammered the first name I could think of, which happened to be Dakota (S. Dakota being the last flag I noticed as I climbed up the chute). I wasn't about to tell another stranger my real name. Boy, is that a mistake I've made too many times. After the Tony G debacle, reckon I finally learned my lesson on that.

FYI: There's a new governor in town. And she makes a mean cup of coffee and bakes cookies in a brick oven on the roof of the capitol, just as any good public servant should.

Her name is Wilma Grace. Governor Wilma Grace. Reckon I might be voting for her if it comes to that.

—Rita/Dakota

Okay, so the dudes who have been chasing me around the last few days are good. I guess this late in the game, we are all A-listers. Attrition and evolution, amirite? They cover each other, know how to keep quiet, look like they've seen a bunch of action flicks and all that.

But I was obsessed with the weather channel. And the Home Alone movies. Just needed the wind to shift. Everything else was already in place. I knew the building they were staying in, was watching them with their daily sweep patterns, trying to find me. I must've killed someone they liked. Relentless, these guys.

The first sign that a breeze was picking up and shifting was the purple balloon overhead, streaming sideways like it was late for work. Me too, little buddy.

Didn't take much to get them chasing me. Right into an alley that dead-ends. Up the fire escape, then kick the ladder away. I was over the roof and gone before they realized they were trapped, the fog coming for them.

Kinda sucks, really. Being this good and not having anyone to brag to.

It's been two weeks since I last wrote. Apologies for the neglect! Wilma and I have been getting to know each other and talking to someone is better than writing to nobody.

Daily routine: Wilma makes breakfast and we plan our day, which mostly revolves around what to eat for lunch and dinner. There are tons of books, but not many good ones. Shelves of leather law tomes that look pretty and will kill your soul if you actually read them.

Most of the offices here are ransacked, paper and folders everywhere. I cleaned one out to make a bedroom, and not gonna lie I looked through all the folders for some UFO secrets. JFK stuff and nuclear codes. It's mostly building permits and the like. As bad as the law books.

There are sacks of unopened mail here. I started going through it. Wilma gave me a fancy letter opener, told me to knock myself out. The things we do to occupy ourselves.

There's calm in routine. I haven't felt this at peace since I escaped the hunter's snare — or rather, since Rita escaped.

Have to keep reminding myself that I'm Dakota now. Mustn't slip up, not once. Wilma and I are building something special here. She let me into her home, and I try to think if I would've done the same if she showed up at Costco. Would I have let her in? Share my space? My supplies? Trusted her as I slept? I'm not entirely sure I would.

Which I guess makes Wilma a better person than me.

Bonanza! Power. Sweet power. All mine! Mwahahahahaaha!

Waited all day to make sure the fuckers coming for me didn't make it home (weather delay!) and then explored their little hidey-hole. They have it all boarded up and padlocked. The system is pretty clever: seven padlocks that make a chain holding a steel door closed. Any key for any of the locks opens the whole thing. A nice little sign of human cooperation and trust.

I tried the zip-pull key I found on the guy who winged me, and sure enough. Friend of theirs. Two locks still unaccounted for. Makes me wonder who else they've lost. Or if they're just away.

Inside, survivor paradise. Wires out the window to what I'm assuming are solar panels on the roof. Water from a rain catchment system that I guess is also up there. That combo meant my first hot shower in ages. An electric coffee maker. A freezer full of food. Guns and ammo for days.

I could live here forever. Okay, kinda sad once I wrote that down. Besides, the place feels like a magnet for people with ill intentions. I mean, it brought me here, right?

Man, has it been a month already? Wilma has a desk calendar, one of those things where you tear off a page each day. The weekdays are wrong, of course, given it's from three years ago. It's not Tuesday, but it is the 17th of August. Wilma is meticulous about keeping track.

She's been here since it happened. Survived by sheer luck, and by locking herself in a closet full of office supplies. She told me she heard terrible noises during the initial aftermath: fighting, dying — both the quick kind and the slow. That explains the bodies in the stairwell. I asked about that, and she went quiet.

Way back after our first dinner, I asked how she came to be governor and she said, "Somebody had to, so I stepped up." Amazing that a person can see a need for something they don't want to do themselves — but they do it anyway.

I had asked if she was in office before, and she laughed. "I was in the office," she said. "More of an admin role."

We'd both benefited from the end of mankind — me avoiding repayment of my student loans, or having to sort out the divorce, Wilma getting one heck of a promotion. After which we talked glass ceilings and gender pay gaps and things I hadn't thought of since the last time I was in the company of another woman, which was I don't know how long ago. All meaningless since the end came.

Shit. Writing this by the window and just saw Tony G looking up at me from below.

Batteries, inverter, hot water heater, I know what these things are but couldn't begin to tell you how any of it works. Nor could I fix them when (not if) something breaks. Crazy how much of the world I always took for granted. So much faith. Electrons pushing through wire and making a TV glow with images fed in from a Nintendo cartridge that only works if I blow on it just right.

Excitebike. Never played it before, but now I spend hours a day on it. Not riding the bike, which gets repetitive, but designing my own courses. Building worlds. Playing God.

If you set a track up just right, the game plays itself. Just hold down the accelerator and every jump sends you down the backside of the next jump, faster and faster to the finish line.

Predestined. Ordained. Free will not needed. Just a flat-out mindless race to the end.

Duck Hunt is here as well with two little plastic guns. Makes me laugh, thinking of the grown men living here together, taking off their big guns at the padlocked door and picking up these.

Pew pew. Electrons smiting ducks.

How the fuck does it all work?

My dad would've liked it here. My mom would've found it confusing as hell. Dad would've dug the wood paneling, the fine art, rubbing shoulders with lawmakers (albeit mostly dead), not to mention his penchant for a framed certificate on a wall.

I explained to Wilma that if Mom were here, she'd get lost in these corridors. How in her last few years she'd have stood like a child in a supermarket and shouted for help. I'd have to calm her down, reorientate her to time and place as if she'd been airlifted and dropped into the middle of a maze. I imagine that's how it was for her in her last days: doorways she didn't recognize, choices she didn't understand. How exhausting that must've been.

Wilma never had a family, and I feel a little bad for her. She'd have made someone a great mom. But things didn't work out that way, and now she has me, and I think she enjoys having me around.

Ha! I was about to write "Life is short" then stopped myself, realizing how ridiculous that would sound, how condescending when there are only a handful of survivors. Better I write "Life is over", or "Life is shit." But I can't quite bring myself to say that either given that I'm sipping a rather lovely sparkling white wine from a crystal champagne flute as I write this.

This world, for those of us left, is a place of contradictions. Stark contrasts between us in here and those out there. Maybe nothing has changed after all.

Gunshots outside my building last night. A reminder that the rest of the world is at war, and not with ducks. Can't stay here forever, I've decided. This journal is a reminder of how dangerous flickering lights are at the top of buildings, however dutifully one tries to draw the blinds shut. A little bit leaks out. Or you forget, and there's a beacon to your excess and good fortune.

I removed all the other locks when I first moved in. Gonna hide my key where only I would think to look. Not gonna write it down here, if you killed me and are pawing through this journal hoping for a clue. Tough luck, asshole. Maybe the place doesn't even exist. Maybe I made it all up to get you looking for the shangri-la of dude dens. Have fun wasting your time.

The truth is, I have a purpose. To right the wrongs of others. Because we aren't the same person in this one life we live. We change over time. Even our deepest habits can change. And I finally get a sense of who we get to be in the afterlife:

Whoever the fuck we want. All of our past selves, all at once. Shifting and morphing like the mist on a swirling day. Old one minute and a child the next. Wise and foolish. Brave and trembling. Walking with our chins up, a smile on our face, tears streaming down our cheeks.

We spent this evening playing blackjack for penny stakes. Wilma cracked open a bottle of Bordeaux she said she'd been saving, which to me tasted like every other red wine I've ever tried, but that she described as 'magnificent'. I said I'd take her word for it and we laughed and then she smiled at me. There are happy moments where I could cry.

At bedtime I douse the lamp and peek through the blinds. Tony G is there. He has a gun, one of those with a scope. He uses it to look up at us, searching the windows for movement.

At times he hides behind a dumpster in an alley across the way — other times he paces back and forth on the stretch of sidewalk opposite, like a crazy man, a caged tiger. Looks as if he's talking to himself.

Wilma says he's tried to get up here, but he's too dumb. She checks the chute and the stairwell barricade regularly, makes sure she isn't followed. Also said he's forever chasing down postcards on balloons like a lunatic, and I swear my heart almost stopped in my chest. Though I didn't let it show.

I haven't told Wilma that it was me who wrote the cards, or that I gave the idea to a very bad man who is now doing the same. I've an odd sense of shame around that. I'm not ready for her to look at me differently, to judge. Will she blame me? Maybe. Will she ask me — tell me — to leave? God, I hope not. Better we don't ever find out.

If I'm careful, and I only go a couple blocks a day, and the wind stays out of the north like this, I'll be there in two days. Give or take. Some of those buildings will be familiar. I've stayed in them before, in a previous life. Know the ins and outs. Or should I say the outs and ins. Always know the outs first. Just in case.

Part of going is to not stay here and waste away. The food wouldn't last forever. Neither would my sanity. People are meant to move, to graze, not be penned up in one place.

And let me be honest for once: I don't think I'm going because I want to save anyone. The same folks I'd be saving are the ones trying to kill me. These days, I pretty much shoot on sight. I guess I've learned not to trust anyone, no matter what they say.

You should too.

Ever since Tony G saw me at the window, now and again we hear him calling out my name. Or rather calling out for the Rita of his postcards (the Rita I've put behind me). Today was one of those days.

The fog was thick. We sat on the roof deck in our lawn chairs, blankets over our knees. Like looking out over cloud tops at 30,000 feet. Clear up here, a cushiony soft layer below that you could almost drop down and land on.

We toasted chunks of Wilma's homemade bread over the flames of the brick oven and dipped them in bowls of gravy. She could tell I had something on my mind — I never was good at hiding my feelings. Guess that's why I never much took to cards. Crappy poker face. An open book.

Wilma said I could tell her anything and it would be alright.

"The postcards," I started to say —

"Ugh. Those damn things." She reached under her chair and pulled out a handful of cards with straggly remnants of string attached. "Nothing but trouble. You know, Dakota, if I got my hands on the person who wrote these, I'd ... I don't know what I'd do."

And that was the end of that.

I'm hiding you now, diary. For reasons that should be obvious to us both.

Costco, next exit. The billboard looms over the side of the freeway promising discounts galore. I try to imagine a going-out-of-business sale. I imagine a thousand balloons released to the sky for some grand opening. Brings to mind all the balloons we drop as politicians give acceptance speeches. Should've told us everything, the way political balloons go down and not up.

This is the dangerous place. The eight lanes of cars. The tall walls meant to keep the road noise from waking the neighbors. The highrise, high-density housing like so many roach motels. Lines of sight everywhere. I'll never see the world the same again after so many hours of peering at it through my scope.

Sometimes, I take my eye away and the black cross is still there. It's there on some lawyer's face one billboard over, asking me if I've been injured in an accident.

Yeah, asshole. You might say that.

Sometimes, diary, we get too comfortable and life has a way of slapping us out of ourselves. Waking us the fuck up. I'm shaking — with anger? Fear? Dread? All of the above. Tony G took it upon himself to send a message to Wilma. Wrapped it around a rock and slingshotted it through a window with a huge CRASH! Only made it as far as the eleventh floor, thank Christ. Any higher and she'd have heard it. As it was, I'd gone to collect files from the twelfth so got to it first.

When I picked it up and unwrapped it and read what he'd written, I searched the street below through the shattered window pane. He was down there alright. Stared right at me. And when he saw I was looking back at him he stretched out his arm and pointed at me. Accusing. Venomous. After which, he ran off.

Can't tell you how freaked out I am right now. That man could ruin everything. Get me evicted from my new home, destroy my friendship with Wilma. If she finds out the truth, I'm fucked. Super fucked. Back out on the street. Then what?

He hasn't found the way in here yet, but he might if he's determined enough, motivated enough. And right now he seems pretty determined and motivated. I'm starting to question if perhaps I should be more proactive about this Tony G situation. And rather than waiting like a rat in a trap for him to come to me, I take steps to prevent it getting that far. Protect what I've come to think of as mine. Can't risk any more of these messages. No siree.

Before I go off to most likely die, might be a good time for some confessions. Five things that'll land me in hell if su

One: es
on G   e
top do

Two: Pr
dead o   st
is no lo

Three: ey
Meyers

Four: I   er
a good

Five:
some   ept
me sane when the world was falling the fuck apart.

She is a
LIAR!

Do Not Trust

Dear diary,

I think I made Wilma a little suspicious of me today.
Totally innocent. I was just trying to surprise her with
a custom luke-warm shower rig (radiator on the roof,
some hose leading down to her shower).

Wanted to make it a surprise, but she caught me coming
out of her office looking guilty af. The last time she
gave me that look was back in the early days, when I
found the wall safe and tried cracking the combo for
shits and giggles. She told me to stop wasting my time.
The safe was empty when she moved in, and she's never
known the code.

Anyway, she liked the gift and we're hoping for
sunny days to get the water warm. But I'm reminded
that living with others means respecting their
privacy. Besides, I've given up on looking for secrets.
Companionship is so much more valuable.

P.S. I've added more chairs to the barricade to keep
Tony G out. First time I've seen it from the top. Way
more bodies in there than I thought. Fuck, people must've
been desperate to get out.

The parking lot is being watched, no doubt about it. You don't lure people into a trap without checking it diligently. So how to get to the building without being seen? Can't even trust moving at night. Costco has an electronics department full of cameras, even ones that see in low light, not to mention batteries for eternity.

The element of surprise is all I have going for me. A day is spent on the uppermost floor of the office building on the east side of the freeway, scanning the world around me and thinking. Office buildings are a good place to wait. Fewer bodies decomposing, better seals on the glass for when the weather turns, and something not many scroungers seemed to have figured out: break rooms. Vending machines. Where the food that never dies sits on their little spiral-fenced balconies peering out through the glass.

If I eat enough shit that never expires, will I absorb the same power?

One can only hope.

Early start. Wilma's leaving to get supplies from the mini mart a few blocks down, just as soon as she's sure Tony G isn't around. I volunteered to go as I have something I need to do, but she insisted she wanted the exercise and the air is clear enough today that it won't bother her chest. I couldn't argue. Didn't want to raise suspicions. So I've come up with a plan B.

Hear me out. I'm going to send the man across the street a message of my own and tell him about the trash chute. I know it sounds crazy, but I have to take control before things go sideways. I can't let him scurry around out there knowing what he knows. He's like a ticking bomb. And I can't wait for him to blow this place up and everything we've worked for. I won't.

I've drawn him a diagram and wrapped it around Lieutenant Governor Schuler's brass nameplate (she won't be needing it anymore). Should grab his attention. A few rubber bands to hold it in place.

As soon as Wilma is out of sight, I'll throw it close to Tony's favorite dumpster. Then all I have to do is wait for him to find his way in. Better this way than wondering every single day, week after week, when he's gonna find it himself.

I see him, the fucker. So far away he's little more than a smudge in my scope, but there he is up on the roof in an orange vest letting a blue dot drift up into the sky. I hover the little black cross on his head, finger twitching, resting on the trigger. No way I could hit him from here. Would be more luck than skill, more God than me. Gravity would curve the bullet down several feet. The wind would push it aside.

It doesn't hurt to dream, though. And even funnier, I imagine shooting the balloon out of his hand just as he's releasing it, so it pops in his face. He'd hear the crack of the rifle some moments later and realize how lucky he'd been. That it could've been him. Almost worth taking the shot, just thinking about it. My finger cramps from doing nothing.

And then he's gone. The blue dot riding the wind, looking for a victim. If I waited long enough I'd spot a hero or two crossing the parking lot myself, disappearing inside, to whatever awaits them there.

Gotta put a stop to this.

While the staff take an extended rest amongst the tables and chairs in the stairwell, I sit in their designated break area on the tenth floor. It's nothing special, but I like to imagine how this place was when the people were here to fill it. Bustling with life and gossip. Folks picking at pasta salads ("It's my own recipe, Margot! Here, try some.") or low-cal yogurts ("Watching my waistline, Joan. You know how it is after menopause!").

In the corner kitchenette is equipment that no longer serves a purpose without power: an empty fridge with its door hanging open, a big espresso machine, a hefty dinosaur of a microwave. At least they didn't end up in landfill, I think with a snort. End-times humor at its finest.

Wilma came home a while ago and is taking a nap. I've got the chute open, listening. I hear him now, diary. The slide of the hatch. Time to execute plan B. Good choice of word there, Dakota: execute.

I see him. Nine floors below, clambering up the flags. Nine floors. There'll be an equation for that, I'm sure. The speed at which things fall over distance. The rate at which that speed increases. How an object behaves differently at greater velocity, feels heavier, more deadly.

I'll leave you under a seat cushion to ponder that, diary. While I give the big old staff microwave one last purpose to fulfill.

BRB.

Genius idea or the death of me, at this point I'm resigned to either. The idea came from watching the wind push a wayward shopping cart that trundled down the slight slope of the side parking lot before crashing into a dumpster. There's a semi scrunched up against the freeway wall on the other side. Climb on the cab, up to the top of the trailer, drop over the wall onto the dumpster, and then get behind it.

After all that, the stupid stuff really begins.

There's a drop-cloth one floor below me in an office that was getting painted when the world ended. And a pair of work gloves that fit real nice. Both are critical parts of this really terrible, stupid, no-good, idiotic plan.

I wanted to move Tony G. No way can we have him stinking up our only route in or out. Ran down to the fourth floor where the Patriot Ladder hangs. Put away my letter opener, which was Plan C if the microwave didn't work: destroy the only way up.

Climbing down, my whole body trembled. Realizing I just killed a man. Brain full of excuses. When I heard him groaning. Not quite dead.

I waited there, just a dozen feet above him. He was looking at me, a sadness on his face, blood everywhere, not long for this world.

"Tried to warn you," he said. The words were soft, the light inside him fading. He seemed resigned to it all. "She's a liar. Not who she says she is."

It was in that moment, clinging to Connecticut, that I realized the note he sent wasn't about me. It was meant for me.

Time to keep detailed notes in case whoever finds my body is the only one who knows what happened.

I got moving around three in the afternoon, grabbing the last creampie from the vending machine on my way out the door. Take this job and shove it.

No contacts crossing the freeway. Footprints on top of the semi told me I wasn't the first person to use this route. Landed pretty hard on the dumpster lid and twisted my ankle. Ominous start.

Sitting behind the dumpster now, marveling at how it doesn't smell much worse than the rest of the world. Is that because everything inside it has rotted away to nothing? Or has the rest of the world gone off and I've gotten used to the stench? Hard to say.

The drop cloth goes over the shopping cart and reaches the ground. My pack and gun go inside the cart. It's a tight squeeze, but I slither through where cases of Coke and toilet paper packs normally go, the shit the cashier comes around to scan by hand.

Gloves on, reaching forward, I can pull myself along the parking lot, a few feet at a time. Now that I know it works, I sit back and wait, eat a creampie, update my journal, until it gets dark.

I helped Tony out of the chute and down to the floor, but he was already past saving. The last thing he did was weakly press his rifle into my hands, but I wanted nothing to do with it. Never want to kill again.

I remember from my explorations down here, looking for a way up, that there were more storerooms. HR looking places buried away from the halls of power. For weeks now I've been practicing filing folders away. Now I rummage and ransack. What I'm looking for has to be here. Proof that he's lying and crazy. But I hear my mom warning me about tells. Something deep inside already knew it was too good to be true.

It takes me less than an hour to locate some personnel records. The folder is open in front of me. Grace, Wilma. Performance reviews. An old resume. A headshot. Of a completely different person.

The woman I've been living with all this time, who is she? And why did Tony G think I shouldn't trust her?

Someone's coming. To be continued.

Nothing suspicious, I hope, about a shopping cart covered in garbage not being where you thought you saw it last. At night. In the pitch dark. In a Costco parking lot.

I pull a few feet and wait. I pull when a breeze flaps the drop cloth. I follow the white painted line just inches from my face. Can't see anything ahead or to either side, but I know the path is clear from scoping the route. When I crash into the brick wall by the loading dock, I nearly shit myself.

Getting out of the cart is noisier than I'd like. Grab my pack and my BFF Buck, steal around toward the truck bays. The good thing about a trap is they're usually unlocked. Welcome mats out.

One last pitstop for some water and a quick note in the journal by headlamp. I take the little plastic lock off the side of the journal and toss it. Won't be needing that anymore.

Grabbing the barrel of a gun before someone shoots you in the face is a good idea, up to a point. Saves your face but not your fingers.

Wilma burst in, eyes fell to the open folder. Face a murderous mask. She raised the rifle. Tony's rifle.

It was the smile that let me know I was about to die. Like her kick was the horror in the eyes of those who had learned to trust her.

The gunshot is deafening. It almost doesn't hurt, not in the moment. Too much pain for any of it to register. Several fingers gone in a cloud. Gonna pass out. Can feel it.

I watch as she rummages in my pocket, finds the journal there. The way she holds it, I know it's not her first time reading it. She knew. All this time. All the secrets I hide.

Almost all.

The letter opener, I keep in my boot.

It's my mom's face I see as I slide it into her neck.

Weeks and weeks of trust and love and hope, spilling out.

Days and days of opening government letters with this thing.

One more package from Uncle Sam to open up before I pass the fuck out.

I follow the sound of whimpering. A man crying. It's coming from the warehouse office. A man in a cage. Must've followed the balloons back to the source, just like I did. Except he was probably expecting a frightened little girl here who needed saving. Didn't know a killer had set a trap.

His eyes bug out when he sees me. Like I'm his salvation. Gripping the bars. Begging me to free him. Hissing at me.

Slow down there, buddy. I'm not here to be a hero. On the desk is a scattering of postcards and little balloons. They're so small without any air in them, before they get stretched out thin and translucent. Hard to believe what they can become. How far they can go. So easy to judge a thing by what it is and not see what it might be.

Footsteps. The man in the cage is pleading with me to save his life.

Clayton, he says his name is.

I tell him to shut the fuck up.

Writing with my left hand is like learning to write all over again. Looks like a stranger's thoughts. Feels like a stranger's thoughts.

I tried trusting someone one more time, and it almost got me killed. No more of that. That Rita is dead. I felt her leave at the same moment the last spark of life left ~~Wilma's~~ that woman's eyes. Trusting in others has always been my undoing. Thinking the world cares if I'm safe or not. It doesn't.

Even now it taunts me with a safe place just a dozen floors above me that I can't reach. No way I'll be able to climb those flags with my hand a useless stump.

My hand will never be the same, but there's one blessing in all of this: I never learned how to shoot a rifle with my right hand. No bad habits to unlearn. I decided to accept Tony's gift. I take it from ~~Wilma~~ the dead woman. No shoulder to cry on, but this wooden stock will have to do. It's a good rifle. Probably deserves a name.

It took keeping a journal for me to realize what they are best for, and that's for setting down our mistakes. Learning from them. So we don't repeat them over and over.

I've learned a lot since the apocalypse began. I've learned that my words can hurt people. Get them killed. I've also learned that try as I might, it's impossible to keep people out of my business.

You are learning both of these things right now. You picked up my journal, didn't you? No lock to keep you out, so in you went. Probably wondering how it ended up on your desk, the same desk where I used to write postcards and tie them up with string.

You see, while I was on my way back to the Costco you stole from me, I too was reading my journal, seeing where things went wrong. All my mistakes. I made plenty of them. The biggest thing I learned was when to keep my mouth shut.

I bet you're curious now. And I hope you're leaning real close when you read this part. I hope your neck is exposed. I hope you're so eager to see where this is going that you don't hear me coming up behind you.

I got you, motherfucker.

-Rita

P.S. Clean-up on aisle nine.

Made in the USA
Middletown, DE
22 August 2024

59609464R00061